John Huntley Skrine, Julius Peter Paul David

Under two Queens

Lyrics Written for the Tercentenary Festival of the Founding of Uppingham

School

John Huntley Skrine, Julius Peter Paul David

Under two Queens

Lyrics Written for the Tercentenary Festival of the Founding of Uppingham School

ISBN/EAN: 9783744766722

Printed in Europe, USA, Canada, Australia, Japan

Cover: Foto ©Andreas Hilbeck / pixelio.de

More available books at **www.hansebooks.com**

CHAPEL AND SCHOOLHOUSE, UPPINGHAM.

UNDER TWO QUEENS

LYRICS

WRITTEN FOR

The Tercentenary Festival of the Founding of Uppingham School

By JOHN HUNTLY SKRINE

AUTHOR OF 'UPPINGHAM BY THE SEA'

εἰς οἰωνὸς ἄριστος ἀμύνεσθαι περὶ πάτρης

London
MACMILLAN AND CO.
1884

For the Vignette on the Frontispiece of Uppingham School Chapel and Old Schoolhouse, I am indebted to the kindness of my friend Mr. Charles Rossiter of Uppingham, who made the sketch for the purpose.

TO

ROBERT JOHNSON

Our Founder

IN REVERENT MEMORY

AND TO

EDWARD THRING

Our Second Founder

IN HONOUR AND AFFECTION

IS DEDICATED

THIS TRIBUTE OF VERSE

Dedicatory

TO

E. T.

Whom in dim years that are done
 Master 'twas honour to call,
Under a kindlier sun
 For a music of festival
Take, in the numbers of one,
 This the love-message of all.

One name ever who heeds
 Will hear in the changing line,
As I tune upon slender reeds
 Songs but the half part mine,
Songs the shadow of deeds,
 Shadow of deeds that are thine.

PREFACE.

THE following Lyrics were written to be set to music as a festival Cantata, which it is intended to perform this summer at Uppingham School among other Tercentenary ceremonies. With the necessary exception of the Dedicatory verses, the Epilogue, and a few stanzas elsewhere, they have been so set by the Author's friend and colleague, Herr Paul David. They are here published separately, in the hope that for a certain circle of readers they may have, apart from their setting, some value also of their own.

It would be much to hope that any one will care to open this volume to whom its subject is not introduced by some personal tie; unless, indeed, the history of an Elizabethan foundation revived in our own age, with circumstances not less distinctive than those of any similar revival, may claim to be of more than local interest. But there are those, perhaps not so very few, whose ear the Author seeks with confidence, sure that they will give his verse a welcome, if it wakens some echo of aims and sympathies of which they are themselves a part, and of which any record will seem good.

CONTENTS.

Part I.

Part II.

Part I.

THE OLD.

ὡς ἐὰν ἄνθρωπος βάλῃ τὸν σπόρον ἐπὶ τῆς γῆς, καὶ καθεύδῃ . . . . καὶ ὁ σπόρος βλαστάνῃ καὶ μηκύνηται ὡς οὐκ οἶδεν αὐτός.

A MARCH.

A.D. 158–.

I.

HAIL, maiden our Queen, right queen of our England,
The maiden of lands, the unconquered, the free,
Since lone 'mid the nations, unmastered, unneighboured,
God isled His fair England, God gave her to thee:
Thrice hail, for thy crown with a glory is kindled,
Old fame of thy fathers, new fame that shall be:
For the voice of our thousands is one to uphold thee,
One heart is the land from the sea to the sea.

II.

Low rumbles war thunder to eastward, to southward;
Shall the lord of the Spains of thy lieges be lord?

B

The spies out of Rome **and the** traitors swarm over :

Shall the Pope have our England ?   Up, banner : out,
        sword !

What ! we, that with Sydney rode, yeoman by noble,

Five spears against fifty, nor counted our lack—

That shook fiery Juan, and grappled fell Parma,

And died in the breach when the Fleming went back—

What ! we, that roved **over** King Philip's own Indies,

And robbed the arch-robber, and flouted the proud—

Shall we fear ?   Be of cheer, O our Queen, **the**
        undaunted ;

Let the storm break and fall, thou shalt **face it**
        unbowed.

III.

When the storm-rack drives leeward, the rainbow
        outspanneth ;

Where cleaveth the ploughshare, there quickens the
        sod :

So breaks the new sun o'er the land we have fought **for,**

So blossom the flowers where our musters have trod.

In the tramp of our war, in the roar of our battle,

There waketh a nation, there dawneth an age :

Praise hast thou, O Queen, in the soldier, the seaman;

But praise shalt thou have in the singer, the sage.

Thy star, that burns red in the war-smoke uprolling,

Shall soften, shall beam on the harvests of peace :

And sure shall men plant in the land of the freeman,

And the good they have sown for their children increase.

A LEGEND OF THE FOUNDING.

1584.

ALL day long till daylight died,
Echoing from the loud hillside,
Down the long green valley rang
Stroke of tool and hammer-clang.
All day long with might and skill
Strongly wrought the builders still;
Drew the line and trenched and hewed,
Master wise and craftsman good,
Shaped the great blocks one by one,
Corner-stone and corner-stone,
All day long till eventide.

Then from eastward valleys wide

Where dark Welland mute, unseen,
Creeps his crumbling banks between,
From the winding willow line,
Over meadows of the kine,
Over uplands of the sheep,
Bringing silence, bringing sleep,
Came the boon night over all.
Came and let the starbeams fall
Soft on dreaming wood and wold,
Mead and tilth and croft and fold,
Fleeces in the glimmering pen,
And the drowsy eaves of men.

Then to one who wandered still,
Musing on the silent hill
By the heapings of the stone,—
Lo! across the midnight blown
Sudden on the trembling air,
High and mystical and rare,
Wild as elfin pipes that flute
Through the waste when eve is mute,

Came a blast of magic **song**
And a chanting rolled along,
And **a** burden strong, elate,
Lofty syllables of fate,
Voices of the Unseen that know
Works of men that fade or grow
In the increasing ages' flow :—

SONG.

" Ye who build on Roët's steep
   Witting not the thing ye do,
Where ye sow shall others reap
   When the old is grown the new.
      Lay the sure foundations deep,
         Strongly **lay** them, lay them true :
      Lo ! there rise when ye shall sleep
      Builders building after you.

" **Large of heart ye shall not lack**
   Guerdon large for toil and gold :

Time shall yield the increase back,
When the new shall crown the old.
Lay the sure foundations deep,
Strongly lay them, lay them true:
Lo! there rise when ye shall sleep
Builders building after you.

"Thrice and thrice and thrice once more
Runs the age of mortal men:
Thrice three months of years are o'er
Then the old is born again.
Lay the sure foundations deep,
Strongly lay them, lay them true:
Lo! there rise when ye shall sleep
Builders building after you."

Ceased the voice, but all the air
Trembling yet the burthen bare;
And the echoes creep and creep
Over uplands of the sheep,

Over meadows of the kine,

O'er the far hill's bounding line,

Thin and thinner, till they die

In the waste of starry sky

And **the** silences on high.

VOICES OF UPPINGHAM TOWER.

A.D. 17—.

Out of belfry windows hoary,
    Wind-beleaguered, we
Watch, O men, your changing story,
    Changing not as ye.
All the ages' mingled treasure
    Hold our hearts in fee :
Days that were our chimes outmeasure
    And the days that be.

Chorus.

Through the town our voices wander,
    Fleet and wander,
    And beyond her
Over silent pastures yonder

Far their echoes range;

Tolling, tolling,

Still out-rolling,

Still to one sure music doling

Time and chance and change.

Round us dwells a simple people,

Scattered far by holt and steeple

Over uplands wide:

These content and little caring

How the eager world be faring

'Mid their herds abide.

Up from Catmos vale ascending,

Slow to midweek market wending,

Troop the mighty beeves;

Troop the fleeces brown and heavy;

And the burly drover levy

Hums about our eaves.

'Neath yon legend-graven portals

Wind the satchel-laden mortals,

Rosy morn or gray :

Mute we list the scholar droning,

List sonorous sage intoning

Half the weary day :

Then we lift the hammer duly,

Strike the sudden noontide truly :—

Ha ! they hear it pealed ;

Outward flings the merry riot,

Shakes the street's contented quiet,

Shakes the laughing field.

Once through Sabbath morns upstealing

Came the fervent, bold, appealing

Voice of long ago.

All too soon, to silence banished,

Fled the voice; **our glory** vanished ;

Died the moment's glow.

Ere our iron tongues grow rusty,

Ageing, ageing in the **dusty**

Glooms of belfry hoar,

Shall this sleepy calm be broken,

Deeds be done, and words be spoken

Hero-like, once more ?

Chorus.

Through the town our voices wander,

Fleet and wander,

And beyond her

Over silent pastures yonder

Far their echoes range ;

Tolling, tolling,

Still out-rolling,

Still to one sure music doling

Time and chance and change.

Part II.

THE NEW.

Exiit ad coelum ramis felicibus arbos,
Miraturque novas frondes et non sua poma.

Not as the flowers that unfold

Does the planting of men decay :
Twice hath our bloom outrolled,
Twice overreddens the spray,
For the Queen we worshipped of old,
For the Queen whom we love to-day.

THE OLD IN THE NEW.

(AN APOLOGUE.)

She.

FAIR son, and wilt thou be gone
    From our old gray towers
To the world of men, and the wild
Far countries over the tide :
Were it not wiser done,
    In our knightly bowers,
Where the line of thy sires, my child,
Abode, thou too to abide?
    Thy fathers, were *they* not bold,
    And loyal each to his lord :
    Not he who in slaughter rolled
    The White Rose back at the ford?
    Yet they by forest and flood,
    'Mid a faithful people, alone,
    Dwelt happy.   O son of their blood,
    And must thou be gone?

He.

I am son of their knightly blood,
 O mother, true son :
But, save I be more than they,
I were least and worst of my line.
For pleasant it were and good
 To live on, live **on,**
By river and lawn and gray
Old towers of the home that is mine;
 But **the** Queen hath bidden her best
 To council and camp and fight;
 And a fire that will not rest
 Has sprung in the land alight;
 And the blood of my sire who rolled
 The White Rose back **at** the ford
 Burns in me.   O now as of old
  We are true to our lord.

CHANGING GUARD.

A COLLOQUY OF THE OLD AND THE NEW.

Genius of the Past speaks.

" HIGH warder of sacred treasure,
    Boon mother of thousand sons,
In my place nine ages I tarry
    Till the fateful glass outruns:
And hark ! there soundeth a summons
    With the last of the falling sand,
Like challenge of good knight's trumpet
    That peals in a lonely land:
And fear is upon me and wonder,
    For a noise of gathering feet
Affrayeth the age-long quiet
    Of the still memorial seat."

The Present.

"O mother of sons, and warder
    Of the holy treasure of time,
Our name it is spelled and written
    In the Fates' eternal rhyme.
Sons whom thou barest never,
    We spring to **thine** ageing line:
We come nor **without** thee nor of thee,
    Thy children, and yet not thine.
And **we** spoil **thee,** O mother, and crown thee,
    And boon we mingle and bane;
For lo! at our coming thou passest,
    And passing thou com'st again."

The Past.

" Right well ye have spelled the riddle
    That winneth my room and state;
Yet one word more there lacketh,
    One token-word of fate.

Ere the golden key I render,
  Ere the mystic door unseal,
Say, how will ye guard my treasure,
  And what is the dole ye deal ?"

The Present.

" As God, the all-equal Giver,
  Free rain and abounding sun,
Or thanked or unthanked, down poureth
  On all, and denieth none :
So we, as the high God help us,
  On the throne of thine ancient hall,
None favouring, none forgetting,
  True measure will mete to all."

The Past.

" It is spoken.   Behold I render
  The key ye shall fear to take :
For the High Ones hear the promise,
  And woe to the lips that break.

But ye, O sons **whom I bare not,**
    Shall wax in my waning light,
For yours is the glad Hereafter,
    But mine the Past and the night.
I pass, as a cloud upgathered,
    As a wraith at the withering morn,
To the silence of things forgotten,
    To the **shadows of** things unborn:
For the great world moveth, moveth,
    With the moving Finger on high,
With the time to be strong and **to labour,**
    With the time to be spent and **die.**"

The *Present.*

" **O not to the** shadow, the silence,
    Shall the light of thy life go down.
Lo! we that unmade remake thee,
    And we that have spoiled **thee,** crown.
Of thy wealth, thy own, thou hast given
    A name, and a space to thrive,

And an altar stone unbroken,
    And an altar flame alive.
And we of our wealth will give thee
    To shine in an ampler morn,
In joy of a spring re-risen,
    In might of a life re-born :
And not to wax old we give thee,
    But yet to endure and reign,
And arise a mother of blessing,
    A mother of truth, again."

Chorus.

A melody new and olden
    Is waked on the silent lyre :
Torch ever on torch enkindled
    Upbears the eternal fire :
From faith that is white in its ember,
    Shall faith in a flame aspire :
For the fathers are turned to the children,
    And the children's heart to the sire.

NEW WINE.

(A RALLYING SONG.)

I.

WHEN the game is keen
On the listed green,
The tearless war of the White and Red;
When far and fleet
Flock racing feet
By down and dingle and brooklet bed;
When the lilied deeps,
Where Welland sleeps,
To the leap and laugh of the swimmer awake;
Or wise and slow
Twain cronies go
By the green lane under the rose-hung brake:

Still round us and over

Are voices that hover

In field or in hall, at the task, at the play ;

And they follow along

Like a haunting song,

Like the wind on our hills that is never away.

For a confident word

Our hearts have heard

Of a dawning hope that it bids achieve,

Of a cause to be loved,

Of a truth to be proved :

And one hath spoken and all believe.

" Old is earth and her hopes are hollow,"

Sing the men in the world out there.

Give us a leader, a leader to follow,

And another song we will teach them here.

O yet and O yet there are crowns to be won

For hearts that venture, for eyes that see :

And there rises a new thing under the sun,

And we, we know it—and who but we ?

II.

From the dim matin bell

Creeping on us to tell

How sweet are our slumbers, how surely to flee ;

Or chirp of the sparrow

By ivy-grown **narrow**

Cell doors, whence we flutter him, drowsy as we :

To the mad steeple blast

That sets evening aghast

When the Muse Elegiac **is** sorest at stand,

Breaking in and pursuing

With wreck and undoing

The numbers reluctant, at point to be scanned—

O from waking to rest,

In earnest, in jest,

There is one thought is lord of our days, of our

nights ;

In the breast of the boy

Is the man's strong joy,

A burden that lifts us, a shadow that lights.

Something, my brothers,

Our own and none other's,

Something we treasure Time shall not forget,

We few and we fameless,

The new and the nameless ;

Ah ! yet they shall know us, shall number us yet.

" Old is earth and her hopes are hollow,"

Sing the men in the world out there.

Give us a leader, a leader to follow,

And another song we will teach them here.

O yet and O yet there are crowns to be won

For hearts that venture, for eyes that see :

And there rises a new thing under the sun,

And we, we know it—and who but we ?

III.

O the days of yore

When a boy might pore

On the scroll of the deeds of a knightly sire,

The frank brave **days**

Of peril and praise,

When faith was simple and hearts were fire,

And 'twas reason high

To battle and die

That a maid was fair or a leader true—

Say, whence and where

Comes wandering here

This waft of the breath of the glory of you.

For **the** droning flute

Of our hinds is mute

At a clarion pealing a point of war,

And our hearts grow hot

With we know not what,

And a glamour runs over the hills afar,

And the days of yore

Are back once **more**

With the simple faith and the selfless deed,

And a knighthood true

Is sworn anew

Of who dare follow who dares to **lead.**

" Old is earth and her hopes are hollow,"

    Sing the men in the world out there.

Give us a leader, a leader to follow,

    And another song we will teach them here.

O yet and O yet there are crowns to be won

    For hearts that venture, for eyes that see:

And there rises a new thing under the sun,

    And we, we know it—and who but we ?

SUN and shower, shower and sun,
   Long you tarry, too long.
Black on our upland the thorn-rows run,
   Black, without leaf, without song.
Seaward yonder the wide land wakes ;
By a hundred waters your wing outshakes,
Leaf by leaf, the pale April flakes :——
   Here you wrong us, you wrong.

Ah ! we know it what sweet amend
   Sweetly the wrong will cure,
When the boon year shines to the mellowing end,
   And the faithful suns endure ;
For late to come shall be late to flee,
And Summer brood on the Autumn lea,
And loth the swallow take wing to sea :——
   So tardy our bloom, so sure.

TERCENTENARY REVISITANTS.

FROM the land of dreamless slumber,
From the silent fold of spirits
And the Meadows of Forgetting,
Half unsealed from sleep
Come our spirits, softly drifted,
With a wingless motion faring,
Lightward, earthward, on.
And across this stirless ocean
Where we float,
As a wind from viewless havens
Cloud-begirt
Ripples out to barks returning,
Strike the airs of home.
Soon, ah, surely soon, the clinging

Golden vapour, morning-smitten,
Shall unclose :
We shall see again the meadow
From the thrifty runlet climb
Up the terraced hill to dewy
Swarded alleys, rose-enwoven,
Where the brown walls rise
Russet-gabled, as we knew them,—
Ah ! but hoar by now with tender
Touches of slow-pacing seasons,
And the wash of rains unnumbered,
Since we slept and all forgot.

*   *   *

Ha ! what glimpses through the breaking
Golden mist ?
Lo ! again a sheeted splendour
Shimmers broad.
Is it Titan shield ? or burning
Fierce flame-buckler of archangel
Over guarded town uplift ?

Nay, we dream ; so sorely dazzles
Earth's new daylight, and so mighty,
Gathering all the dawn upon it,
Springs and spreads a roof majestic
O'er a shrine we knew not ours.
Gleam the white walls massy-buttressed,
Age-proof, deep :
And by tower and hall upspringing,
Bower and lawn,
Stately grown beyond our knowing
Spreads our ancient home.
Yea, and hark ! from echoing doorways
Rolling outward, rolling upward,
Soars a music, glad, acclaiming,
As of men that after battle
Joying chant the might of heroes,
Chant the daring and the doing,
And **the** cause that overcame:—

Song.

I.

On the lonely plain, by the sounding main,
    Through the heart of the midnight hours,
There **pealed a music unearthly** clear,
So wild a **breath of delight and** fear
That the wide field shook and the stars **to hear,**
    And the hoarse deep hushed afraid :
Till the dawn broke red on a hundred towers,
And a rampired wall, and a prince's bowers,
On a nation's pride and embattled powers—
    Such music the Gods had made.

II.

Through the long dim years, in silence, in fears,
    With labour unpraised, unknown,

We wrought, we ventured, a fameless folk;
For we hearkened a music that inly spoke,
And to measure we builded, and stroke by stroke
    The home of our faith arrayed :
Till the bright noon smote through the cloud o'erblown,
And lo! in her height our city upgrown,
From base to summit our own, our own—
    Such music a faith had made.

III.

Through the shining sky a storm drew nigh;
    Our wall with an earthquake rent.
Sing sorrow, sing sorrow, for hopes that fall!
—But over us echoed a trumpet call,
And a free wind sang through the tottering hall,
    With a breath as of ocean foam.
And forth to the wilds before us sent
The march of the deathless music went,
And builded anew with might unspent
    For the homeless people a home.

D

IV.

Then Ho ! for the song divine and strong,
  And the wall to the music reared !
And Ho ! for the storm and the wind and the wave,
And the deathless melody **strong** to save,
And the hand on the helm, and the joy of the brave,
  When the angry seas run high—
The joy of the brave to have dared and steered,
With the surge on the deck and the surf in the beard,
Right on, right on, till the reef was cleared,—
  To have dared, and not to die.

EPILOGUE.

JUST are the heavens, it is written, and man as he
    soweth shall reap.

Aye, but a hundredfold oft by the grave of the sower asleep

Quickens the harvest, and teems overflowing, and
    whitens afar,

When the fulness of tarrying seasons is rained from a
    kindlier star.

Did they dream it who gave of their treasure, and
    careful for ages to be

Laid stone upon stone, bidding rise fair houses of
    learning and free—

Did they dream it, how others should graft where they
    planted, man perfecting man,

And the bloom of a spring unimagined out-blossom the
    years that foreran ?

Nay, who that hath **lent unto Time may** forereckon
    the fruit of his loan ?

As the need of their day was **they did, and their**
    morrow hath cared for its own.

What rose of our spring **shall we** gather this morn for
    the grave of a sire **?**

What sheaf shall we bind **from his** furrow ?   What
    voice of remembering **lyre**

Shall **bear him** love-tribute of children, and break——so
    the living **may** dare——

The silence undreamable, holy, the **peace of the**
    heavenward air ?

Bidding hail——from who cherish the light that he lit on
    the wind-trodden wold,

Where he laboured, and rests from his labours, true
    shepherd, nor far from his fold :

Bidding hail,——for his light shall not out, but a purpose
    unsleeping, **unworn,**

Keeps watch, wedding age unto age ; and the heirs of
    his spirit are born :

And the voice of him speaks from the silence more
    clear, and the hand of him dead
On ways that he living beheld not hath beckoned a
    brother to tread :
And the rose-red of hope interwoven is one with the
    memories gray
Of who sleeps in the dust of ten ages, who lives in
    the deeds of to-day.

So greet we the dead. But the living we greet not ;
    their praise be His due,
His only, All-worker, All-helper, Who teacheth man's
    fingers to do.
His the praise : but the love be thine also, fair Home,
    whom we greet without fear,
Paying nursing-dues back of our love, pious coin of
    our hearts that revere ;
Fair home of our spirits, dear hearth where the fire,
    the undying, had birth,
Which we bear from the motherland altar on sunder-
    ing pathways of earth,

One ember each son in **his** bosom : it fails not who
    faileth not it,

And there burns on his far away altar the **flame of his**
    boyhood relit ;

Pure flame of a worship remembered, a faith with his
    seasons upgrown,

Truth kindled from lips of another, blown bright by a
    passion his own.

And ever about him brave words of the foretime as
    oracles ring,

Sooth-speakers, live words of the live heart that bred
    them, the lips that gave wing—

" Not the praise, not the prize, be thy guerdon, O son,
    not the pride of the strife ;

But to render the fruit of thy soul to the sower, the
    life for the life."

So ring they, true omens that fail not, betray not, sure
    pilots of doom,

Many-winged on earth's ways that are many. And
    one in the pent city gloom,

In the labour-smoke rolling, the whirl, the uproar of
the labour-vexed air,

Hears their echo outsounding the clamour, and knows
to endure and to dare,

Helping men as man helped him of old. And another
in isles oversea,

Planting England afar and the manhood of England
in kingdoms to be,

Sees the mute endless pasture no longer, but sees
through the mist of his eyes

Faint, faint, the green ivy, gray wall, and the threshold
familiar arise.

And one on wild hills by the camp-fire remembers, as
silently grow

The stern iron hours that bring nearer the morning,
bring nearer the foe;

When a name of thy names shall shine upward, clear
flame in the fierce battle breath,

Or a life of thy nursing drop earthward, thee honour-
ing, O mother, in death.

Lo! now there is festival light on the holy
    memorial hearth ;

The Boon Mother has bidden her children, and hallows
    the **feast** of her birth.

There is pause for an hour in the march of her climb-
    ing unwearying years,

There is crowning of labour, and singing of deeds, and
    forgetting of tears.

For the nine silent ages **are** over, the tenth to its
    measure hath run,

She hath heard the new errand of Time, **and** arisen
    and ventured and won :

She hath travailed and seen of her travail, hath tasted
    of doubt and dismay,

Hath bent to the storm and re-risen ; and now, in the
    calm of her day,

Soft droop the still folds of her banner, by sunlight of
    honour caressed,

Since they tossed in the battle-rank o'er us and peril
    went by them and blessed.

She rests, the Boon Mother, and gladdens, and garners
the fruit of her days :

She rests, with her sheaves in her bosom. But out over
untrodden ways

Range onward her questioning eyes, and of Time the
oncoming require—

" Shall the morn be as yesterday good, shall the
children be true as the sire ?"

What omen shall hearten us, brothers, what word **make**
the ranks of us strong,

As the shout of a king in our muster ? Make answer
and fear not, O song,

Make answer—" One omen is best, for **the** fatherland
fighting to stand,

For the fatherland ever, **the** walls that engird **the**
inviolate land ;

For the laws that upbuilt her, uphold **her,** the corner-
stone mightily laid,

The truth **that is** life of her life, and the faith that
endured **unafraid** ;

For the word that she **spoke ere** another, the vision
　　she knew for her own,

The paths she trod foremost, the honour that **crowns**
　　not or crowns her alone;

For the brotherhood strong, the live bulwark, the
　　watchword that secretly runs,

The great hope——on the lip it is silence, is fire in the
　　breast of her sons;——

And for memories fair of **who once** were beside us,
　　and nevermore they

Are beside us, **howe'er they be** of us; who loved her
　　and saw not her day;

Leal hearts, and they trusted her fortune unshapen,
　　her star ere it shone,

And they watch from the twilight of souls, and their
　　joy with **our** joying is one.

Yea, one omen is best, and to us it has fallen, we hail
　　it our own,

And bold are our **feet** on the pathway, the dim, the
　　untravelled, unknown;

For life answereth life, on the Future are mighty the
hands of the Past,

From the root is unfolded the fruit, from the strong
cometh sweetness at last:

As to-day is shall yet be the morrow . . ."

But over the **preluding string,**

Ere the fire can be voice, ere the **burden be shapen,
the pæan** outring,

There sweeps a hand not of the singer, and ears **of the**
singer have heard

A whisper that hushes his music and **dumbs, as it**
rises, the word:

"Seal surer the dream in the bosom; nor doubt it nor
utter in air:

For veiled as a bride is the morrow," it saith, "as **a
bride** she is **fair.**"

ENVOI.

To P. D.

Go from him who bred you,
    Rhymes—my task is o'er,—
Go to who shall wed you
    To **sweeter chords** and more.

Trust him : he will render
    Love to me in you.
Trust, for he is tender,
    Be he ne'er so true.

Fledgeling rhymes that flutter,
    He will **imp** your wing :
What ye scant can utter,
    That will teach you sing.

Brother's breath with brother
Blows one fire aflame.
Hark! the notes are other,
Yet the voice the same.

NOTES.

Page 18. "That with Sydney rode . . ."

The allusions to Zutphen, Rymenant, and Antwerp, appropriate to the eve of the Armada, are here introduced by a slight and, it is hoped, an admissible anachronism before the "Legend of the Founding."

Page 20. "All day long . . ."

The old schoolroom of Uppingham was built by the **Founder,** Archdeacon Johnson, Rector of Luffenham, in 1584.

Page 22. "Roët's steep."

Roët or Rût is the eponymous hero of Rutland.

Page 23. "Thrice three months of years . . ."

The school, founded in 1584, began to be remodelled thirty **years** ago, or nine generations later.

Page 26. "Yon legend-graven portals."

The old schoolroom stands near the church tower, and opening upon the churchyard. Over the door are faded inscriptions in Latin, Greek, and Hebrew.

Page 27. "Once through Sabbath morns . . ."

Jeremy Taylor became Rector of Uppingham in 1637-38. After the outbreak of **the** Civil War, when he joined the King at Oxford, his living **was sequestrated** by the Parliament.

Page 33. "**Changing** Guard."

An attempt, for which indulgence may fairly be asked, to sketch **the** relations of the original Foundation to the Second Foundation (as it may be called) which began thirty years ago, and to indicate some of the ideas by which the latter has been directed.

Page 33. "In my place nine ages I tarry . . ."
See note to page 23.

Page 46. "We shall see again the meadow . . ."
By way of note on these lines the reader is referred to the frontispiece.

Page 48. "On the lonely plain . . ."

> "That strange song I heard Apollo sing,
> While Ilion like a mist rose into towers."
>
> TENNYSON, *Tithonus.*

Page 49. "Through the shining sky a storm drew nigh . . ."
The reference is to the exodus of the school in April 1876, when, on account of fever at Uppingham, the school was removed to Borth, on the Cardigan coast, and remained there till May 1877.

Page 51. "Fair houses of learning and free."
"A faire, free grammar school," is the description of Robert Johnson's foundation in the old record.

Page 52. "Where he laboured . . . nor far from his fold."
Robert Johnson was for fifty years Rector of North Luffenham, near Uppingham. His monument is in North Luffenham Church, where he is buried.

Printed by R. & R. CLARK, *Edinburgh.*

www.ingramcontent.com/pod-product-compliance
Lightning Source LLC
Chambersburg PA
CBHW022155020726
47496CB00008B/2729